Memory's Edge:

A Psychological Thriller

By

Richard Trillion Mantey

Table of Contents

Dedication

This book is dedicated to those who have ever felt lost within their own memories…

To those who have questioned what is real and what is merely remembered…

And to the brave souls who choose to face their past, no matter how fragmented, painful, or uncertain it may be.

Because within the fragments of memory…

lies the power to reclaim your truth.

Acknowledgments

This book exists because of the invisible threads that connect thought, memory, and human experience.

To those who have ever questioned their past, wrestled with their identity, or searched for truth within uncertainty—this story is for you.

To the readers who dare to explore the depths of the mind, thank you for your courage and curiosity.

To the thinkers, creators, and visionaries who continue to challenge perception and expand understanding—your influence is deeply felt within these pages.

And to the quiet moments of reflection, where ideas are born and truths reveal themselves—this book owes you everything.

Chapter 1: The Return

A Town Forgotten

In the heart of a desolate landscape lay a town shrouded in mystery, known only to a few as Ravenswood. Once vibrant and bustling with life, its streets now echoed with silence, broken only by the whispers of the past. The crumbling buildings told stories of forgotten dreams and hidden secrets, with every cracked window and weathered door a testament to the lives that once thrived there. As the sun dipped below the horizon, casting long shadows, the town seemed to breathe a sigh, as if it were haunted by the memories it could not escape.

Ravenswood was a place where time stood still, and its inhabitants had vanished without a trace, leaving behind nothing but empty homes and lingering questions. Those who ventured near spoke of an oppressive weight in the air, a feeling that something was always watching. The townspeople who had once shared laughter and sorrow were now ghosts, their stories buried beneath layers of dust and neglect. The sense of isolation was palpable, wrapping around any visitor like a cold blanket, urging them to leave before the darkness enveloped them.

Among the town's many enigmas was the old library, a relic of a bygone era that seemed to hold the key to Ravenswood's dark past. Its shelves, filled with forgotten tomes and yellowed newspapers, whispered tales of tragedy and betrayal, revealing a history that the town desperately wanted to forget. Curiosity drew a few brave souls to its doors, but those who dared to delve into its depths often found themselves entangled in the very secrets they sought to uncover. The library had become a sanctuary for the lost, a place where time intertwined with memory, and the boundary between reality and illusion blurred.

As the protagonist, a weary journalist searching for the truth, stepped into Ravenswood, she felt an unshakeable connection to the town. The more she explored, the more fragments of her own past began to surface, intertwining with the town's haunting history. Memories she thought were long buried resurfaced, bringing with them a cascade of emotions and a sense of urgency. The deeper she dug, the more she realized that the answers she sought were not just about the town but also about herself, revealing a tapestry of intertwined destinies that could not be unraveled without consequences.

In this town forgotten by time, the past was not as distant as it seemed. The echoes of Ravenswood called out to her, urging her to confront the truths she had long avoided. As she pieced together the puzzle, every revelation threatened to upend her understanding of the world around her. The suspense escalated, revealing that in Ravenswood, what was once lost had the power to change everything, reminding her that some memories are never truly gone, waiting patiently to be unearthed and faced, no matter the cost.

Ghosts of the Past

In the dim light of her childhood home, Jessica felt the weight of memories pressing down on her. Shadows danced on the walls, reminiscent of the laughter and tears that once filled the air. Each creak of the floorboards whispered secrets of the past, tales she thought she had buried deep within her. Yet, as she began to sift through old photographs and dusty boxes, the ghosts of her past crept back, uninvited but persistent, demanding to be acknowledged.

The town she returned to was small, but its history loomed large, wrapped in layers of intrigue and denial. Jessica discovered that the very streets that held her childhood memories were also haunted by the unresolved traumas of its residents. The more she delved into the past, the more she realized that nothing was as it seemed. Her friends, once trusted allies, now bore the weight of dark secrets, their smiles hiding the betrayal that had marked their lives.

As Jesica pieced together fragments of her memory, she encountered the specter of her sister, who had vanished years ago under mysterious circumstances. The question of her disappearance loomed over Jessica's investigation, twisting her perception of those around her. Each revelation felt like a knife, cutting deeper into her psyche, challenging her grip on reality. Memories became unreliable, and the line between truth and illusion blurred, igniting a sense of paranoia that made her question everything she thought she knew.

The deeper Jesica dug, the more she unearthed unsettling truths, each one more shocking than the last. Her childhood home, once a sanctuary, transformed into a prison of nostalgia, trapping her in a maze of recollections. Friends turned into foes, and allies morphed into enemies, as Jessica realized that betrayal was woven into the very fabric of her past. Each encounter felt like a game of chess, where every move could lead to a revelation or a downfall, heightening the suspense and tension.

Ultimately, Jessica's journey through the ghosts of her past was not just about uncovering hidden truths but also about confronting her own demons. The path to understanding was fraught with peril, revealing the depths of human psyche and the lingering effects of trauma. As she stood at the edge of her memories, Jessica knew that the past would never truly leave her; it was a haunting reminder that some secrets refuse to fade away, waiting patiently to be discovered, or to destroy those who dare to unearth them.

Chapter 2: Whispers in the Walls

The Old House

The old house stood at the edge of town, its weathered facade bearing witness to decades of secrets and memories long buried. Vines crept up its walls, intertwining with the peeling paint, as if nature was trying to reclaim what had been lost. It was a place that whispered of laughter and sorrow, a repository of the past that beckoned to those who dared to remember. For many, it was merely a relic, but for a few, it was a haunting reminder of choices made and paths not taken.

Inside, the air was thick with dust and a lingering scent of decay. The floorboards creaked underfoot, each sound echoing like a distant memory. Shadows danced in the corners of the dimly lit rooms, where sunlight struggled to penetrate the grime-streaked windows. Here, time felt suspended, as if the house itself was holding its breath, waiting for someone to unlock its doors and reveal what lay hidden within.

As the protagonist stepped through the threshold, a chill ran down their spine. They could almost hear the echoes of past conversations, the laughter of children long grown, and the heated arguments that had shattered the silence. It was here that the lines between reality and memory began to blur, where the past seemed to bleed into the present. Each room held its own story, a fragment of a life once lived, yet now forgotten.

But the house was not just a vessel of nostalgia. It was a labyrinth of deception, where every corner turned could lead to a hidden truth or a darker secret waiting to be uncovered. The more the protagonist explored, the more they felt the weight of unseen eyes watching, the pressure of time urging them to uncover the mysteries that lay shrouded in the shadows. It was a race against memory, where every revelation could either heal or further shatter their already fragile psyche.

In the end, the old house stood not only as a backdrop for the unfolding drama but as a character in its own right, embodying the themes of trauma, memory, and the ghosts of the past that refuse to be exorcised. As the protagonist faced the truths hidden within its walls, they realized that some memories never truly leave; they remain, lurking just beneath the surface, waiting for the right moment to resurface and demand to be reckoned with.

Uninvited Memories

In a small town where whispers of the past linger like shadows, uninvited memories often surface at the most unexpected moments. Marissa stood frozen in her living room, a long-forgotten photograph slipping from her fingers. The image, frayed at the edges, depicted a group of familiar faces, but one stood out— a figure she had tried to erase from her mind. The sight of that smiling face ignited a torrent of emotions, dragging her into a whirlwind of nostalgia and dread, as the echoes of a past she thought was buried clawed their way back to the surface.

As the days passed, Marissa found herself haunted by the resurfacing of these memories. Each time she closed her eyes, she was transported to a summer long ago, where laughter and joy mingled with a chilling undercurrent of deceit. The lines between what she remembered and what she chose to forget began to blur, creating a disorienting maze of recollections. It was as if the town itself, with its creaking houses and overgrown gardens, conspired to remind her of the truth she had buried deep within her psyche.

The more she tried to push these memories away, the more persistent they became. Shadows danced at the corners of her vision, whispers echoed in the silence, and the photograph seemed to call out to her, urging her to confront the darkness she had hidden for so long. Marissa's nights were plagued by vivid dreams, each one revealing fragments of a story she thought she controlled. With every dream, the urgency grew, and she realized that some secrets would not remain hidden, no matter how hard she tried.

Seeking solace, Marissa turned to her childhood friend, Jake, who had always been the keeper of their shared memories. However, as they reminisced, Jake's demeanor shifted, revealing layers of tension and unspoken truths. The conversation took a turn when he mentioned the incident that had forever altered their lives—the moment that had caused the rift in their friendship and the town's collective memory. It was a moment that had been shrouded in silence, but now it demanded to be remembered, forcing Marissa to confront the reality of her past.

As the town's secrets began to unravel, Marissa understood that uninvited memories were not simply remnants of a forgotten past. They were the keys to understanding the present and unlocking the truth hidden beneath layers of denial and fear. In her quest for clarity, she realized that exposing these truths would require courage, not just to face her demons but to embrace the reality of what had never truly left her. With each step she took, the past loomed larger, and the stakes grew higher, leading her deeper into a labyrinth of betrayal and revelation, where every memory held the power to change everything.

Chapter 3: The Unraveling

Secrets Beneath the Surface

In the quiet town of Willow Creek, the past lingers like a shadow, waiting for the right moment to resurface. Secrets lie hidden beneath the facade of normalcy, where every resident harbors a story they dare not share. The air hums with unspoken truths, and the once-vibrant community is now a tapestry woven with threads of deceit and denial. As the layers of history begin to peel away, the chilling realization dawns that some memories are never truly forgotten.

Amelia, a local journalist, finds herself drawn to the eerie legends surrounding the town's abandoned quarry. Whispers of its dark history echo in her mind as she delves deeper into the lives of the townsfolk. Each interview reveals unsettling connections to a long-buried tragedy, and Amelia becomes increasingly aware that her own past is tangled in this web of lies. The more she uncovers, the more she questions her own memories, leaving her to wonder if the truth will set her free or ensnare her further.

As Amelia's investigation intensifies, she discovers a network of relationships built on betrayal and revenge. Old friendships fracture under the weight of new revelations, and the once tight-knit community starts to unravel. Each character she encounters seems to guard a fragment of the truth, but their motives are shrouded in ambiguity. The suspense thickens as Amelia realizes that the answers she seeks may come at a devastating cost.

In a race against time, Amelia grapples with her own unreliable memories, battling the specter of her past that refuses to let go. The line between reality and illusion blurs, as the town's secrets begin to manifest in ways she never expected. As she gets closer to the heart of the mystery, she must confront her own demons and decide how far she is willing to go to uncover the truth.

Ultimately, the revelations that surface challenge everything Amelia thought she knew about herself and those around her. As the final pieces of the puzzle fall into place, she faces the haunting question: can one ever truly escape the shadows of the past? With each twist and turn, the story reveals that some secrets are best left buried, and the price of uncovering them may be more than one is willing to pay.

An Unexpected Visitor

The door creaked open, revealing a silhouette shrouded in shadows. Kim felt her heart race as she recognized the figure standing in the dim light of her living room. It had been years since she had seen him, yet the familiarity of his presence sent a chill down her spine. Memories flooded back, uninvited and disturbing, as she recalled the evening that had forever altered her life. With each step he took forward, she felt the weight of the past pressing down on her, threatening to unravel the carefully constructed facade she had built.

"I didn't think I'd ever see you again," she managed to whisper, her voice almost lost in the thick tension that filled the room. He smiled, but it was a smile that held no warmth, only a promise of chaos lurking beneath. The air grew heavy with unspoken words and suppressed emotions, each second stretching into an eternity. As he stepped into the light, his eyes glinted with a knowing that made her stomach churn. It was as if he had come not just to revisit old wounds but to reopen them with a vengeance.

Their conversation began with pleasantries, but Kim could sense the underlying currents of deceit and manipulation. He was probing, testing the boundaries of her fragile composure. Each question he asked felt like a calculated move in a game where the stakes were her sanity. She fought to maintain her grip on the truth, aware that her memories had become unreliable over time. Yet, she couldn't shake the feeling that he knew more than he was letting on, and the implications of that knowledge were suffocating.

As the hours slipped by, the atmosphere shifted from tense to outright hostile. The fragments of their shared history were like shards of glass, cutting deeper as they revisited the past. Kim's mind raced, piecing together moments she had buried, but his presence made it impossible to think clearly. It was as if he had come to collect a debt—one that she had long thought settled. Each revelation he dropped was like a breadcrumb leading her back to a dark place she had fought to escape.

In the end, Sarah found herself standing at a crossroads, with her past and present colliding in a dizzying whirl. The unexpected visitor was not just a ghost from her past; he was a harbinger of the chaos that had once consumed her life. As he turned to leave, the finality of his words echoed in her mind, leaving her with a haunting question: how much of her life had been dictated by the shadows of memory, and could she ever truly escape their grasp?

Chapter 4: Fractured Truths

A Glimpse of Clarity

The air was thick with unspoken words as Clara stood at the edge of the town's forgotten cemetery, her heart pounding with a mix of dread and anticipation. She had returned to the place that haunted her childhood memories, a town where secrets lay buried alongside the dead. With every step she took, the weight of her past pressed down on her, whispering reminders of the trauma she had tried to forget. Yet, as the wind rustled through the trees, it felt as though the ghosts of her past were beckoning her to uncover truths she had long buried.

In the distance, an old oak tree stood sentinel over the graves, its gnarled branches reaching out like skeletal fingers. Clara approached it, remembering the summer days spent playing in its shade, unaware of the darkness that lurked beneath the surface. This tree had witnessed her childhood innocence shatter, a silent witness to the betrayal that had twisted her family's narrative. As she placed her hand on the rough bark, a surge of memories flooded back, vivid and raw, each one more disturbing than the last.

Her mind raced with fragmented images of that fateful night—the argument, the screams, the finality of silence that had fallen over their home. It was a night that had changed everything, yet Clara had never allowed herself to confront the truth. Instead, she had built walls around her heart, convinced that forgetting was the only way to survive. But now, standing amid the echoes of her past, she realized that clarity could only be found by facing the shadows she had long evaded.

As the sun dipped lower in the sky, casting an eerie glow over the cemetery, Clara felt a strange sense of resolve. She had come to understand that the past was not just a series of events to be concealed; it was an integral part of who she was. The secrets of her family, the lies that had festered over the years, needed to be unearthed. With a deep breath, she resolved to confront her memories, to delve into the murky waters of her mind and uncover the truth that had eluded her for so long.

With renewed determination, Clara stepped away from the cemetery, her heart lighter than it had been in years. She understood that clarity was not just about uncovering hidden truths but also about embracing the pain that came with them. As she walked through the winding streets of her childhood, she felt a shift within herself, a movement towards healing. The journey ahead would not be easy, but for the first time, she was ready to confront the darkness, to face what had never really gone away, and to finally reclaim her narrative from the shadows.

The Lies We Tell

Lies are the threads that weave through the fabric of our lives, often binding us to the past in ways we cannot fully comprehend. In the small town of Havenwood, whispers of deceit lurk in every shadow, and the truth is a precious commodity, carefully guarded by those who fear what it might reveal. As memories fade and twist, the stories we tell ourselves take on a life of their own, morphing into something unrecognizable. Each character in Havenwood carries their own burden of lies, creating a tapestry of suspicion and fear that envelops the community.

At the center of this web is Mia, a woman haunted by fragmented memories that refuse to align with her reality. She grapples with the lies she has told herself about her past, convinced they offer her protection, even as they threaten to unravel her present. As she delves deeper into the town's dark history, the lies begin to surface, pulling her into a vortex of betrayal and revenge. The more she uncovers, the more she realizes that the truths she seeks may be far more dangerous than the lies she clings to.

The people of Havenwood are experts in deception, each harboring secrets that could shatter the delicate balance of their lives. As

Mia's investigation unfolds, she encounters a cast of characters whose own lies intertwine with hers, leading to unexpected alliances and treacherous betrayals. The tension mounts as loyalties shift, revealing the lengths to which individuals will go to protect their own narratives. With every twist, the line between truth and deception blurs, challenging Mia to confront the ghosts of her past.

As Mia digs deeper, she begins to question her own memories and the reliability of her perceptions. The psychological tension escalates, reminiscent of the works of authors like Gillian Flynn and Paula Hawkins, where the past is a haunting presence that refuses to fade. With each revelation, Mia must navigate a landscape filled with unreliable narrators, where even her own mind becomes a source of uncertainty.

Ultimately, "The Lies We Tell" serves as a powerful exploration of how deception shapes our identities and relationships. In Havenwood, the truth may be elusive, but the impact of the lies we tell is undeniable. As Mia confronts the reality of her situation, she must decide what is worth holding onto and what must be let go. In a world where the past never truly leaves, the journey towards truth becomes a perilous endeavor, one that could either liberate or destroy her.

Chapter 5: Digital Shadows

Hacking Reality

In the heart of a seemingly tranquil town, secrets fester beneath the surface, waiting for the right moment to emerge. The protagonist, grappling with fragmented memories of a traumatic past, begins to uncover a web of deception that connects her to the town's dark history. Each clue she unearths pushes her deeper into a psychological maze, where reality blurs with her memories, leaving her questioning her own sanity. The past is not merely a ghost; it is a living entity, one that refuses to be buried and is intent on revealing itself in the most unexpected ways.

As she delves deeper into the mystery, the protagonist discovers that technology plays a crucial role in unraveling the truth. Cyber intrusions and digital footprints lead her to unexpected revelations about the people she thought she knew. The town's facade of normalcy begins to crack, revealing a sinister underbelly where betrayal and revenge thrive. With every revelation, she grapples with the haunting notion that her memories may not only be unreliable but also deliberately manipulated by those around her.

The tension escalates as the protagonist confronts not only the external threats but also her internal demons. Flashbacks haunt her, intermingling with the present, creating a disorienting experience where the lines between reality and memory dissolve. The reader is taken on a slow-burn journey through her psyche, feeling the weight of her despair and determination. Each twist and turn serves to deepen the sense of suspense, as the stakes become increasingly personal.

In a small town where everyone has something to hide, trust becomes a rare commodity. The protagonist's relationships are tested, revealing the fragility of human connections in the face of unresolved trauma. As she pieces together the puzzle, the reader is left to ponder how much of one's identity is shaped by the past. The theme of memory resurfaces repeatedly, reminding us that what was once buried can come back with a vengeance, reshaping our reality.

Ultimately, "Hacking Reality" is about more than just solving a mystery; it explores the complexities of the human mind and how memories, both true and false, can manipulate our understanding of the world. As the protagonist races against time to uncover the truth, the reader is drawn into a psychological thriller that lingers long after the final page. The revelation of hidden truths becomes a catalyst for transformation, leaving the audience to question the nature of reality itself, and what it means when the past refuses to remain in the shadows.

The Code of Deception

In the dim light of the old library, secrets danced like shadows on the walls. The air was thick with the scent of aged paper and the whispers of the past. Caroline sat at a long mahogany table, the flickering candlelight illuminating her troubled features. She had come to this small town seeking clarity, but as the memories began to resurface, she found herself caught in a web of deception that threatened to unravel everything she thought she knew.

Each book she opened seemed to hold a piece of the puzzle, yet the more she read, the more questions emerged. The townsfolk, with their knowing glances and hushed conversations, were not as welcoming as they appeared. Caroline felt the weight of their scrutiny, as if they were all part of an unspoken pact to keep the truth buried. The code of deception ran deep, and she was determined to break it, even if it meant confronting her own fractured memories.

As she dug deeper, Caroline discovered a chilling connection between her family and a series of unsolved crimes that had plagued the town for decades. The line between memory and fabrication blurred, leaving her questioning the reliability of her own mind. With each revelation, she grappled with the haunting realization that some truths are better left hidden. The shadows of her past loomed larger, pushing her closer to the edge.

Caroline's investigation took a dangerous turn when she stumbled upon a hidden diary, filled with entries that hinted at betrayal and revenge. The author, someone she had trusted, revealed a tangled history that intertwined with her own. In a race against time, she had to decipher the code of deception before it swallowed her whole. The stakes were high, and the truth was more elusive than she could have ever imagined.

In this small town where every face was familiar yet every smile concealed a secret, Caroline was no longer just a visitor. She was a player in a deadly game, where the past refused to stay buried. The code of deception was unravelling, but with it came the risk of losing everything she held dear. As the final pieces fell into place, she realized that the greatest betrayal came not from others, but from within herself.

Chapter 6: Ties That Bind

Bonds of Betrayal

In the quiet town of Eldridge, bonds are both a source of comfort and a veil for the darkest of betrayals. As the sun sets, casting long shadows over the familiar streets, the townspeople go about their lives, blissfully unaware of the secrets lurking just beneath the surface. Each neighbor holds a piece of the puzzle, yet the truth remains elusive, cloaked in layers of memory and denial. This is a landscape where every smile may mask a hidden agenda, and every friendship could be a fragile thread poised to snap.

Among these tangled relationships is Sasha, a woman grappling with her past. Haunted by fragmented memories of her childhood, she struggles to discern reality from the echoes of trauma. As she delves deeper into her own psyche, the once-familiar faces of her friends become unrecognizable, each interaction tinged with suspicion. Sasha's journey to uncover the truth leads her to confront not only the betrayals of those she loves but also the betrayals she has inflicted upon herself.

The arrival of a mysterious figure from Sasha's past reignites long-buried fears and unresolved conflicts. This enigmatic presence stirs a whirlwind of emotions, forcing Sasha to reevaluate her relationships and the choices she has made. With every revelation, the bonds that once seemed unshakeable begin to fray, revealing the fragility of trust. As she navigates the murky waters of betrayal, the lines between friend and foe blur, leaving her questioning the motives of those closest to her.

In a town where everyone knows each other's business, the truth can be a dangerous weapon. As Sasha edges closer to the truth, she uncovers a web of deceit that extends far beyond her personal struggles. The fabric of the community is woven with lies, and the stakes are raised when she realizes that revealing the truth could cost her everything. Yet, in the depths of betrayal, she finds an unexpected strength, a determination to reclaim her narrative and confront the ghosts that have haunted her for too long.

Ultimately, "Bonds of Betrayal" explores the psychological complexities of memory and trust, inviting readers to ponder the darker aspects of human relationships. In a world where the past is never truly gone, the journey to uncover hidden truths becomes a gripping tale of suspense and revelation. As the final pieces of the puzzle fall into place, the impact of betrayal ripples through the lives of those involved, leaving indelible marks that may never heal.

Trust in Question

In the small town of Everwood, whispers of betrayal linger like a fog, clouding the minds of its residents. Trust, once the foundation of their close-knit community, now feels fragile, teetering on the brink of collapse. As memories of past grievances resurface, characters navigate the treacherous waters of their relationships, each harboring secrets that could shatter the fragile alliances they've built. With every revelation, the question of who can be trusted becomes increasingly murky, leading to a perilous game of deception.

At the heart of this struggle lies Claire, a woman grappling with her own unreliable memories. Haunted by the shadows of her past, she begins to question her own reality, unsure of who to believe or what to remember. Her journey is a slow burn, filled with moments of tension that unravel the very fabric of her existence. As she delves deeper into her memories, the lines between truth and fiction blur, leaving readers questioning the reliability of what they perceive.

The presence of technology in Everwood adds another layer of complexity to the narrative. Cyber intrigue weaves through the plot, as characters utilize digital means to manipulate and conceal their truths. Secrets hidden in the virtual world reflect the darkness lurking in the hearts of the townsfolk. This exploration of trust in the age of technology raises pertinent questions about the authenticity of connections in a world saturated with information and deception.

As the story unfolds, the characters are forced to confront their pasts, revealing how trauma shapes their present. Each twist and turn compels them to reassess their loyalties and the very essence of their relationships. The suspense amplifies as alliances shift and betrayals come to light, illuminating the complexity of human emotions intertwined with memory and trust. Every revelation feels like a punch to the gut, leaving readers breathless with anticipation.

Ultimately, "Trust in Question" serves as a chilling reminder that the past never truly leaves us; it echoes in the choices we make and the bonds we forge. As Claire and the residents of Everwood navigate their intertwined destinies, they discover that the journey toward understanding and forgiveness is fraught with peril. The lingering question remains: can trust be rebuilt once it has been broken, or is it a bond forever lost in the shadows?

Chapter 7: The Edge of Memory

Lost Time

The clock in the small town of Eldridge seemed to tick differently, each second stretching into an eternity filled with memories both wanted and feared. Nadia, freshly returned after a decade away, felt the weight of the past in every corner of her childhood home. Shadows whispered secrets, and familiar faces bore the marks of time, yet the air was thick with unspoken truths. It was as if the town itself was holding its breath, waiting for her to uncover what had been lost, and what never truly left her.

Days turned into weeks as Nadia attempted to piece together her fragmented memories. The townsfolk were polite, but their eyes told a different story—curiosity mixed with caution. She learned quickly that time had not healed all wounds; some had festered, buried under layers of silence and denial. Each encounter felt like a thread pulling her closer to a truth she both desired and dreaded. The more she dug, the more she unearthed a network of interconnected lives and hidden resentments that had long been dormant.

As the past resurfaced, Nadia stumbled upon a forgotten diary belonging to her late mother. The pages, yellowed with age, were filled with scribbles that hinted at dark family secrets and hidden relationships. The words danced before her eyes, revealing a narrative of betrayal and loss that had been carefully concealed. With each revelation, Nadia found herself drawn deeper into a web of deceit that seemed to implicate not only her family but also the very fabric of Eldridge itself.

The deeper Nadia delved, the more she realized that time had a way of distorting reality. Memories that once felt clear began to blur, casting doubt on her own recollections and the motives of those around her. Friends became foes as she learned that everyone had something to hide. The tension in the air grew palpable, and the town began to feel like a ticking time bomb, ready to explode as old grievances and unhealed wounds resurfaced.

In a final confrontation, Nadia stood at the edge of the town's forgotten history, the truth laid bare before her. The revelations not only changed her understanding of her past but also reshaped her present. As she faced the ghosts of her childhood, she realized that lost time was not merely about the years that slipped away but about the moments that shaped who she had become. With newfound clarity, Nadia understood that some memories are inescapable, and the journey to reclaim them was the only way to truly find herself again.

The Weight of Remembrance

In the quiet town of Eldridge, the weight of remembrance hung in the air like a dense fog. Each street corner held whispers of the past, tales left untold that lingered in the minds of its inhabitants. The residents, with their well-formed routines, often found themselves haunted by memories that refused to fade. It was as if the shadows of their pasts were woven intricately into the fabric of their everyday lives, reminding them that some truths are never truly buried.

As the protagonist, Clara, navigates her own turbulent memories, she realizes that each recollection is a thread connecting her to the town's dark secrets. The more she delves into her own psyche, the more she uncovers layers of trauma that intertwine with the lives of those around her. Clara discovers that the past is not just a collection of memories but a living entity that shapes the present. Her journey becomes a psychological labyrinth, filled with unreliable narrators and deceptive truths.

The tension escalates as Clara's investigation into a long-forgotten tragedy stirs buried emotions within the community. The residents, initially reluctant to confront their shared history, begin to reveal fragments of their own stories, each one adding to the unsettling tapestry of the town's collective memory. Clara learns that the weight of remembrance is not just a personal burden; it is a shared experience that binds the community together in unexpected ways.

As she pieces together the puzzle, Clara faces the haunting realization that some memories are better left undisturbed. The deeper she digs, the more she questions her own recollections and the reliability of those she once trusted. This slow-burn suspense reveals not only the dark undercurrents of Eldridge but also the fragility of human memory, where the past can twist and turn into something unrecognizable.

In the final throes of her investigation, Clara must confront the truth about herself and the town she thought she knew. The revelations are explosive, shattering the illusions she clung to for so long. Ultimately, the weight of remembrance is not just a burden; it is a catalyst for healing and understanding, as Clara learns that embracing the past is essential to reclaiming her future.

Chapter 8: Confronting the Past

Revelations in Darkness

In the quiet town of Eldridge Hollow, shadows seem to whisper secrets that the light cannot illuminate. As the sun sets, the familiar streets transform into a labyrinth of memories long buried. The air thickens with an unsettling tension, as if the very walls of the houses hold their breath, waiting for the truth to resurface. This is a place where the past doesn't just linger; it haunts, waiting for the perfect moment to unveil its dark revelations.

Amelia, the town's reclusive librarian, finds herself drawn into the undercurrents of Eldridge Hollow's history. With every book she uncovers, she discovers fragments of lives intertwined with her own. Each page turned is a step deeper into a maze of deceit, betrayal, and unfulfilled promises. The deeper she delves, the more she realizes that the town's seemingly mundane facade hides a tapestry of trauma that connects its inhabitants in ways they cannot yet comprehend.

As Amelia grapples with her own fractured memories, she encounters figures from her past that she believed were long gone. Shadows from her childhood emerge, forcing her to confront the truth of her family's shattered legacy. With each revelation, the lines between reality and memory blur, leading her to question everything she thought she knew about herself and the people around her. In this psychological dance, trust becomes a dangerous game, and every ally has the potential to become an enemy.

The tension escalates when a series of unsettling events unfold, threatening to expose the town's darkest secrets. A mysterious figure lurks in the background, orchestrating a chilling game of cat and mouse. As the town's facade begins to crumble, the residents are pushed to their limits, revealing the hidden fractures in their relationships. The revelations come like thunderclaps in the stillness, shaking the very foundation of Eldridge Hollow and forcing its inhabitants to confront the demons they've tried to forget.

In this intricate web of suspense, the question remains: can Amelia uncover the truth before it consumes her? "Revelations in Darkness" is a testament to the idea that some memories are never truly gone. As the past resurfaces, it becomes clear that the journey to uncover the truth is fraught with peril, and the only way forward is to confront the darkness that has always been lurking just beneath the surface.

The Price of Truth

In the small town of Eldridge, the weight of buried secrets hung heavy in the air, suffocating the fragile trust among its residents. As the sun dipped below the horizon, casting shadows that stretched like the past itself, whispers of truth began to unravel. For those who had lived with the ghosts of their memories, the price of uncovering the truth seemed too steep. Each revelation felt like a raw wound, reopening scars that had long been hidden beneath the surface of everyday life.

Claire, a journalist drawn back to her hometown after years away, found herself at the center of a mystery that intertwined her own history with the dark tales of those around her. Every corner she turned, every face she recognized, reminded her of the trauma that had shaped her youth. As she peeled back the layers of her own memories, she realized that the truth had a way of changing perspective, revealing not just the events that transpired, but the motivations behind them. The deeper she dug, the more the town's facade crumbled, exposing the raw, unfiltered emotions beneath.

Yet, the pursuit of truth came with a price. With each piece of information Claire uncovered, she felt the weight of the town's collective guilt pressing down harder. Friends became foes, and loyalties shifted like sand beneath her feet. The very people she once trusted began to reveal their true colors, and Claire found herself questioning not only the reliability of those around her but the reliability of her own memories. In a town steeped in psychological tension, the line between truth and deception blurred, leaving her in a constant state of unease.

As the past resurfaced, Claire confronted the haunting specters of betrayal and revenge that were intricately woven into the fabric of Eldridge. The revelations that emerged were not merely about the town's history but also about the personal demons that each resident carried. It was a painful reminder that the truth, while liberating, could also be devastating. Claire grappled with the realization that some truths were better left buried, particularly when they threatened to unravel the very essence of her identity and those she loved.

In the final moments of her journey, Claire stood at the precipice of understanding, contemplating whether the truth was worth the chaos it might unleash. The memories she had fought so hard to reclaim were now a double-edged sword, capable of slicing through the very fabric of her existence. As she prepared to face the consequences of her discoveries, she understood that the price of truth was not just the revelations themselves but the irrevocable change they would bring to her life and the lives of those around her. In Eldridge, the past was never truly gone; it lingered, waiting to be acknowledged, and demanding to be faced head-on.

Chapter 9: A Game of Manipulation

The Puppet Strings

In the quiet town of Eldridge, the past lingered like a shadow, influencing the lives of its residents in ways they could hardly comprehend. Among them was Julia, a woman haunted by fragmented memories of a childhood that had been marred by darkness and betrayal. Each night, she would find herself waking from dreams that felt more like memories, filled with faces and places she could barely recognize. The whispers of a past she thought she had escaped began to seep into her waking life, pulling her closer to the truth she had long buried.

As Julia delved deeper into her own history, she discovered that the strings of her life were intricately woven with those of others in the town. Each person she encountered seemed to hold a piece of the puzzle, a fragment of a larger story that connected them all. The more she learned, the more she realized that the secrets hidden in Eldridge were not just her own; they belonged to everyone. The tension mounted as she navigated a web of deception, where trust was a luxury few could afford.

A chance meeting with an old friend from her past triggered a cascade of revelations that left Julia questioning her own sanity.

The friend, once a confidant, now seemed to be an unreliable narrator, leading her down paths filled with uncertainty and fear. Memories began to blur with reality, and Julia found herself caught in a psychological labyrinth where every corner held another hidden truth. The lines between friend and foe blurred, and paranoia gnawed at her, leaving her isolated and desperate for clarity.

As events unfolded, Sarah uncovered a sinister plot that had been brewing beneath the town's surface for years. It became evident that Eldridge was not just a backdrop for her story; it was a character in its own right, with its own motives and dark secrets. The puppet strings that controlled the townsfolk had origins steeped in trauma and manipulation, revealing that the past had never truly left. With each twist, Julia was drawn deeper into a world where the stakes were higher than she had ever imagined.

In the chilling climax of her journey, Julia faced the puppeteer— the one who had pulled the strings all along. Confronting the truth required not only courage but also a willingness to accept the painful memories that shaped her life. With the past laid bare and the strings cut, Julia emerged transformed, ready to reclaim her narrative and confront the ghosts that had haunted her for far too long. In Eldridge, the shadows may fade, but the echoes of memory would always remain, a testament to the enduring power of the human psyche.

Strategies of Control

In the quiet town of Briarwood, the strategies of control are woven into the very fabric of everyday life. Secrets linger in the shadows, and the past is never truly buried. As residents navigate their daily routines, they are often unaware of the invisible threads that bind them to one another. The manipulation of memory and perception creates a tapestry of lies, where trust is a rare commodity. Each interaction is a delicate dance, a game of power where those who hold the past can shape the future.

Among the key players in this psychological chess match is the enigmatic Claire, who has mastered the art of subtlety and deception. Her strategies are not overt; instead, they rely on the quiet influence of suggestion, drawing others into her web without them even realizing it. Claire's past is shrouded in mystery, and as she returns to Briarwood after years away, she brings with her the ghosts of unresolved trauma. Her return is a catalyst for long-buried truths to resurface, forcing the townspeople to confront the darkness that has lingered just beneath the surface.

Claire's methods are particularly effective in a community where everyone is connected, and the stakes are personal. The townsfolk have their own secrets, and Claire's presence threatens to unravel the delicate balance they have maintained. As she navigates old friendships and rivalries, her strategies become a study in psychological manipulation. She uses her knowledge of others' pasts against them, revealing hidden fears and buried regrets that serve her purposes.

Yet, control is a double-edged sword. As Claire orchestrates her plans, she begins to realize that the past is not as easily manipulated as she believed. Unforeseen consequences arise, and the strategies she employed to exert control start to backfire. The town's secrets, once a means of power, begin to unravel in unexpected ways, revealing the fragility of her carefully constructed facade. The tension escalates as she grapples with the realization that memory, once manipulated, can also reclaim its power.

In the end, the strategies of control in Briarwood highlight the complexities of human relationships and the weight of history. As Claire confronts the repercussions of her actions, it becomes evident that the past can never be fully controlled or forgotten. The revelations that come to light challenge the very foundations of trust within the community, leaving readers questioning who truly holds the reins. The psychological thriller unfolds, demonstrating that sometimes, what we try to bury never stays buried for long.

Chapter 10: The Final Unraveling

The Truth Exposed

In the quiet town of Eldridge, secrets festered beneath the surface like a hidden wound. As the sun set behind the dilapidated buildings, shadows stretched long and deep, whispering of the past. It was here that Sarah Johnson began to unravel the truth about her family's legacy, a truth buried under layers of memory and denial. Each step she took echoed with the weight of unanswered questions, as if the very ground beneath her feet was urging her to dig deeper.

Sarah's investigation led her to the town's archives, where dusty files revealed stories of betrayal and loss. The names of her ancestors danced off the pages, their fates intertwined with the dark history of Eldridge. Yet, as she pieced together the fragments, a chilling realization struck her: the past was not merely a collection of forgotten tales but a living entity that shaped the present. The whispers of those long gone began to seep into her mind, blurring the lines between reality and memory.

As Sarah delved deeper, she discovered that some truths were meant to stay hidden. The more she uncovered, the more she felt the presence of an unseen force watching her every move. The town, with its quaint façade, transformed into a labyrinth of deception, where every friendly smile masked ulterior motives. Shadows danced in the corners of her vision, hinting at the dangers that lurked just out of sight. Trust became a rare commodity, and paranoia seeped into her thoughts like a slow poison.

Her journey was not just about uncovering family secrets; it was a battle against the demons of her own mind. Sarah grappled with her unreliable memories, questioning what was real and what a figment of her imagination was. Each revelation brought her closer to the heart of the mystery but also deeper into a psychological abyss. The truth, once sought after, became a double-edged sword, cutting away at her sanity as she wrestled with the ghosts of the past.

As the final pieces fell into place, Sarah stood at the edge of a precipice, confronted by the ultimate truth of her existence. The revelations were staggering, reshaping not only her understanding of her family but also her perception of herself. In that moment of clarity, she realized that some memories should never resurface, and some truths were buried for a reason. The past, she learned, is an inescapable shadow, forever intertwined with the present, and the only way to heal was to confront the darkness head-on.

Shadows Fade

In the small town of Eldridge, shadows lurked in every corner, a reminder of past secrets that refused to fade. The air was thick with memories, and the residents often found themselves haunted by the choices once made. For Rachel, returning home after years away stirred up emotions she thought she had buried. The old house, with its creaking floors and peeling wallpaper, whispered stories of betrayal and loss, urging her to confront the ghosts that lingered in her mind.

As Rachel navigated the familiar streets, she couldn't shake the feeling that someone was watching her. The gaze of the past was heavy on her shoulders, reminding her of the friendships that had soured and the love that had turned into something dark. Each encounter with the townsfolk revealed layers of hidden truths, as if they were all players in a game she had never wanted to join. The tension simmered beneath the surface, a slow burn that ignited her curiosity and dread in equal measure.

Late one night, while sifting through old photographs, Rachel stumbled upon a picture that sent shivers down her spine. It was a snapshot of her and her childhood friend, Claire, but something was off about it. The smile on Claire's face seemed forced, and the shadows around her appeared deeper, almost alive. A sense of foreboding enveloped Rachel as she recalled the last time they had spoken—an argument that had severed their bond and left scars on both their lives.

Determined to uncover the truth, Rachel began digging into Claire's past, only to find that the secrets had festered like an untreated wound. With each revelation, the line between friend and foe blurred, and Rachel realized that the real danger lay in the memories she had repressed. The town had its own narrative, one that twisted and turned with every new discovery, revealing how interconnected their lives truly were.

As the shadows began to fade, Rachel confronted the reality of her choices and the lasting impact they had on those around her. The final pieces of the puzzle fell into place, unveiling a truth both shocking and liberating. In the end, it was not just about uncovering the past, but about finding the strength to move forward, leaving the shadows behind while acknowledging that some memories would never truly fade away.

Chapter 11: Aftermath

Echoes of the Past

The air was thick with the scent of nostalgia as Anna wandered through the old town, each step echoing with memories that felt both familiar and foreign. The dilapidated houses, once vibrant, stood as silent witnesses to the secrets buried within their walls. She could almost hear the whispers of her childhood friends, their laughter intertwining with the rustling leaves, a haunting reminder of what they had lost and what they had hidden away. It was as if the past was a living entity, watching her, pulling her deeper into its grasp.

As she approached the old library, the heart of the town's forgotten stories, a chill ran down her spine. The building loomed ahead, its windows like eyes peering into her soul, demanding she confront the truths she had long avoided. Memories of late-night discussions and secrets shared in hushed tones flared in her mind, but with them came the weight of betrayal.Anna knew the library held more than just books; it contained the threads of her past, the very fabric of her identity, and perhaps the answers to questions she had never dared to ask.

Inside the dimly lit room, dust motes danced in the shafts of light, much like the fleeting moments of clarity she often experienced. Each book she touched seemed to reverberate with a pulse, as if alive with the energy of those who had come before her. The shelves felt like a labyrinth, each corner hiding a fragment of a memory, a truth that could either bind her or set her free. The deeper she delved into the pages, the more she felt the echoes of her past merging with her present, blurring the lines of reality.

But with every revelation came the weight of uncertainty. Was her memory reliable, or had it been tainted by the trauma she had endured? The faces of her past flickered through her mind like shadows, each one holding a piece of the puzzle she desperately needed to solve. The question loomed: how much of what she remembered was real, and how much had been crafted by her mind to shield her from the pain? The ghosts of her childhood were not just memories; they were specters that haunted her every thought.

As she left the library, clutching a book that felt like it held the key to her past, Anna realized that the echoes of the past would not be silenced. They were a part of her, woven into her very being, and she could no longer run from them. With renewed determination, she vowed to uncover the truth, no matter how painful it might be. The town, with all its dark secrets, was ready to reveal what had never truly left, and Anna was prepared to face the shadows that had shaped her into who she was today.

Moving Forward

As the sun dipped below the horizon, casting long shadows over the quiet town, Mary felt the weight of her past pressing down on her. Memories she thought were buried resurfaced like restless spirits, demanding her attention. Each familiar street corner and dilapidated building whispered secrets of a time she had desperately tried to forget. The unease settled in her chest like a stone, reminding her that moving forward meant confronting the ghosts of her history.

In the days that followed, Mary began to piece together fragments of her fractured memories. The once comforting familiarity of her surroundings now felt suffocating. Each encounter with old friends, now strangers, ignited unresolved tensions and unspoken questions. She realized that the truth had a way of weaving itself into the fabric of her life, a relentless force that would not be ignored. It was time to unravel the threads of deception that had bound her for so long.

Determined to uncover the hidden truths, she sought out the people who had once played pivotal roles in her life. Conversations turned into interrogations as she probed for answers, each revelation leading to more questions. The small town, with its dark secrets, became a labyrinth of betrayal and intrigue. With every layer she peeled back, the realization hit her harder: some memories were not just forgotten; they were deliberately suppressed, lurking just beneath the surface.

As the tension escalated, Sarah found herself entangled in a web of lies, where trust was a commodity more valuable than gold. Each twist in her journey revealed the fragility of human connections and the devastating consequences of buried truths. She began to understand that moving forward required not just facing the past but also reckoning with the impact of her choices on those around her. The stakes were higher than she had anticipated, and the clock was ticking.

In the climactic moments that followed, Sarah stood at a crossroads, understanding that the only way to truly move forward was to embrace her past. The journey had transformed her, igniting a fierce determination to reclaim her narrative. As she took a deep breath, ready to confront the final truth, the shadows of her past began to recede, revealing a path illuminated by newfound clarity. With each step, she shed the weight of her memories, finally prepared to face whatever lay ahead.

Chapter 12: A New Beginning

Healing Wounds

In the quiet town of Eldridge, wounds run deeper than the skin. Beneath the surface, the memories of past traumas linger like ghosts, haunting the residents who try to move on. As secrets unfold, it becomes apparent that what was thought to be buried is, in fact, very much alive. Each character carries their own scars, both visible and hidden, that shape their actions and decisions as tensions rise and trust erodes.

The protagonist, Sarah, finds herself drawn back to the town she left behind, compelled by a mixture of nostalgia and dread. The familiar streets evoke memories she would rather forget, yet they beckon her with an unsettling familiarity. As she navigates her return, she begins to uncover the layers of deceit surrounding her childhood, revealing that the wounds of the past are not only her own but also intertwined with those of her friends and family. Each revelation pulls her deeper into a web of intrigue where every person she thought she knew is hiding something.

As Sarah reconnects with old acquaintances, the theme of betrayal emerges. Friends become foes, and allies are not what they seem. In this small town, everyone has a story, and every story has a secret. The psychological tension escalates as Sarah grapples with her unreliable memories, making her question her own sanity. The more she uncovers, the more she realizes that healing is not a straightforward path; it is fraught with setbacks and unexpected twists that lead her to confront the darkest corners of her mind.

The presence of technology adds another layer of complexity; cyber intrusions reveal personal histories that were believed to be safely tucked away. As Sarah delves into her investigation, she discovers that the digital footprints left behind can weave a narrative just as twisted as the memories she struggles to piece together. The intersection of past and present becomes a battleground as she fights not only for the truth but also for her own sense of self amidst the chaos of revelation.

In the end, healing wounds is not merely about finding closure but embracing the scars that define us. Sarah learns that the past may never truly leave us, but it can inform our future if we allow it. The journey through Eldridge is one of transformation, where each step taken brings her closer to understanding the delicate balance between memory and reality. As the final truths are laid bare, the question remains: can one truly heal when the past continues to echo in the present?

The Future Unwritten

In the stillness of a small town, shadows from the past linger like ghosts in the alleys. The air is thick with unspoken secrets, memories that refuse to fade, and a sense of foreboding that clings to every corner. Characters, shaped by their histories, wander through a landscape that feels both familiar and unsettling, grappling with the weight of choices made long ago. It is in this environment that the future becomes a battleground, where each decision holds the potential to unearth buried truths.

Technological advances have intertwined with the fabric of this town, creating a delicate balance between safety and vulnerability. Cyber intrigue runs rampant, as the characters find themselves not only battling their inner demons but also the external threats that come from a world increasingly dominated by digital footprints. The past, intertwined with modern technology, opens doors to revelations that were once thought sealed. The future, however, remains unwritten, filled with uncertainty and the possibility of betrayal.

As the narrative unfolds, the reader is drawn into a slow-burn suspense that heightens with each twist. Memory itself becomes a character, unreliable and shifting, leading to a deeper exploration of trauma and its effects. The protagonist must navigate through a web of deceit and manipulation, where the line between friend and foe blurs. Each encounter is layered with tension, hinting at secrets that could unravel everything they thought they knew.

The town's dark secrets are not only a backdrop but a catalyst for change, forcing characters to confront their pasts. The weight of memories can be a double-edged sword; while they provide insights, they can also trap individuals in cycles of regret. The future is not merely a continuation of the past but a chance to reclaim agency, to redefine oneself in the face of overwhelming odds. The question lingers—what would they be willing to sacrifice to rewrite their destinies?

In this psychological thriller, the interplay of the past and the future creates a rich tapestry of suspense. As the characters delve deeper into their own histories, they uncover hidden truths that challenge their perceptions of reality. The future is indeed unwritten, but with every revelation, it becomes clearer that it is shaped by the choices made today. The climax hovers on the horizon, promising a confrontation that will change everything and compel the reader to reflect on the nature of memory, identity, and the enduring impact of the past. It's a beautiful day

Author Richard Trillion Mantey

Author Biography

Richard Trillion Mantey is a visionary storyteller, psychological thinker, and transformational voice in modern literature. Known for crafting narratives that do more than entertain, he writes to awaken—blending emotional depth, psychological insight, and powerful storytelling into unforgettable experiences.

His work explores the unseen forces that shape human behavior: the subconscious mind, memory, identity, and the silent stories people carry within. Through his writing, Richard challenges readers to question not only the world around them—but the beliefs, memories, and internal narratives that define who they are.

With a unique ability to merge suspense with self-discovery, his stories resonate on multiple levels—captivating the imagination while provoking deep introspection. Each book is designed to leave a lasting imprint, not just as a story remembered, but as a perspective transformed.

Driven by the belief that words create reality, Richard Trillion Mantey continues to build a body of work that is timeless, thought-provoking, and emotionally powerful—stories that linger long after the final page is turned.

www.ingramcontent.com/pod-product-compliance
Lightning Source LLC
Chambersburg PA
CBHW051334150726
47997CB00004B/1461